HANNAH AND THE TOMORROW ROOM

Hannah leans against the door frame. She chose the yellow for the ceiling. She chose the blue for the walls. It's the first time she's chosen anything like this.

'My tomorrow room,' she whispers.

Hannah's new bedroom is almost ready. Tomorrow, she can move out of the room she shares with her sisters and into a special place of her own. But sometimes things don't go as planned, and someone else needs Hannah's room.

Hannah thinks up some plans to get that 'someone else' out. But it's not as easy as she thinks . . .

A third inspiring story about Hannah, from the author of *Skating on Sand* and *Hannah Plus One*.

Praise for *Skating on Sand*:

'Gleeson paints a sensitive picture of a young child pluckily holding to her own priorities . . . and in the process growing a little in her awareness of the wider world.'
Australian Bookseller and Publisher

Also by Libby Gleeson

Novels

Eleanor, Elizabeth

I am Susannah

Dodger

Love Me, Love Me Not

Refuge

Skating on Sand

Hannah Plus One

Picture Books

One Sunday

Big Dog

Where's Mum?

Mum Goes to Work

Uncle David

Sleeptime

The Princess and the Perfect Dish

The Great Bear

Non-fiction

Writing Hannah: On Writing For Children

Libby Gleeson

HANNAH AND THE TOMORROW ROOM

Illustrated by
Ann James

PUFFIN Books

Puffin Books
Penguin Books Australia Ltd
487 Maroondah Highway, PO Box 257
Ringwood, Victoria 3134, Australia
Penguin Books Ltd
Harmondsworth, Middlesex, England
Penguin Putnam Inc.
375 Hudson Street, New York, New York 10014, USA
Penguin Books Canada Limited
10 Alcorn Avenue, Toronto, Ontario, Canada, M4V 3B2
Penguin Books (N.Z.) Ltd
Cnr Rosedale and Airborne Roads, Albany, Auckland, New Zealand
Penguin Books (South Africa) (Pty) Ltd
5 Watkins Street, Denver Ext 4, 2094, South Africa
Penguin Books India (P) Ltd
11, Community Centre, Panchsheel Park, New Delhi 110 017, India

First published by Penguin Books Australia, 1999

3 5 7 9 10 8 6 4 2

Cover designed by Debra Billson, Penguin Design Studio
Typeset in Australia by Midland Typesetters, Maryborough, Victoria
Made and printed in Australia by Australian Print Group, Maryborough, Victoria

National Library of Australia
Cataloguing-in-Publication data:

Gleeson, Libby, 1950– .
Hannah and the tomorrow room.

ISBN 0 14 130512 6.

I. James, Ann. II. Title.

A823.3

www.puffin.com.au

Contents

The Tomorrow Room   3

A Change in Plans   9

School   17

Plan One   23

Plan Two   30

Cornered   40

Plan Three   45

The Advertisement   53

Assembly Item   59

The Phone Calls   65

Grandpa   72

Family Conference   78

The Tomorrow Room   84

For the kids of Wilkins Public School, Marrickville
— L. G.

For Freya
— A.J.

Hannah

Our baby's called Megan. Dad calls her Ginger Meggs because of her hair. Mum calls her Meggie-gorgeous and kisses her all over.

Lena and Sue call her Chubby Chops or Wet-bum.

I'm the one who chose Megan for her name, and when our grandpa calls her Baby or Bubba I say, 'Her name is Megan.'

Mum says a kid in her class at school was still called Bubba by his family when he was as big as his dad.

It's funny how the same person has lots of names. It's like I say Grandpa but some kids say Pop and some Grandad and Annie says Grandy and Toula says Papou and Tui says Ông Nội.

Chapter One
The Tomorrow Room

'*W*hen can we move in?'

Hannah is sitting on the step of the new added-on room. Her room. Hers and Megan's.

Her father steps slowly across in front of her. He is holding a long pole with a paint-roller on the end and he pushes it hard against the ceiling. A wide, straight road of yellow shows where he's been.

Hannah's mother is on top of the ladder, painting the part where the wall meets the ceiling. She is frowning, concentrating, directing the paint in a tiny track ahead of her brush. There are yellow spatters on her nose, on her arms and in her hair.

'When we finish here,' she says, 'and the smell of paint stops. Maybe tomorrow.'

Hannah leans against the door frame. Tomorrow. She chose the yellow for the ceiling. She chose the blue for the walls. It's the first time she's ever chosen anything like this. 'My tomorrow room,' she whispers. Four whole walls to cover with her posters, and no one to say she can't. She knows already where she will stick up the whales, the puppies and the striped tiger cubs. She can see her shells on the window-sill, her blue 'first' ribbon for the three-legged race at the athletics carnival pinned to the curtain, her paintings stuck on the wall. Everything where she chooses. She wants to sit there, looking at it forever.

Crying baby sounds come from her parents' room down the hall.

'Go and give her a pat,' says Mum. 'I can't stop here yet.'

Hannah goes into their bedroom and bends over the cot. Megan is tangled in her knitted blanket. Her face is as crumpled as a pug puppy. She has sucked the ribbon of her teddy bear and the soggy, pale-blue mass is caught between her tiny fingers.

'What's up, crinkly face?' says Hannah.

The crumples disappear in a gummy grin.

'If you had a tail, it'd wag,' says Hannah.

Megan reaches up and Hannah puts her hands under the baby's armpits. She pulls her upright and then half lifts, half drags her to the edge of the cot. She's never fetched her out of bed before.

Sue comes to the bedroom door.

'What are you doing?'

'Mum said I have to get her.'

'You'll just drop her.' Sue comes over and tries to push Hannah out of the way.

'Mum told me to.'

'You're too little.'

Megan is crying. Hannah's hands grip her tightly. Sue grabs Hannah's fingers and pulls them back. Hannah tries to elbow her out of the way.

Sue takes hold of Megan's legs and lifts them
high over the wall of the cot. Hannah steps away
from her, still holding Megan under the arms.
The baby's head bumps against the cot bars.
She screams.

'Now see what you've done,' says Sue.

'I didn't do it. You did.'

Footsteps come quickly along the hallway.
Hannah and Sue, still holding onto their little
sister, turn as their mother comes into the room.
She frowns. She sweeps the baby up onto her
shoulder, patting her, kissing her head and
murmuring softly as she waves the other two
girls out of the room.

After lunch, Hannah sits in the middle of the new
room with Megan on her lap. They watch their
parents painting.

'See,' Hannah says to the baby, 'this is our tomorrow room. The best room in the house. Just you and me and not Lena and Sue. We're going to put a sign on the door, and it'll say "No twins allowed." They'll have to ask us.' She stretches her legs out in front of her. The floor is covered with painting drop-cloths and the plastic makes crinkling noises under her skin. Megan laughs.

'Hi, Ginger Meggs,' says Dad. He's getting more paint on the roller.

'Can you manage?' says Mum.

'We're fine,' says Hannah. She points to the window. 'My bed will be there and your cot can go on the other side, near the door. And I'm going to stick up all my paintings from school and the posters. And you can have a mobile and Mum'll make some curtains.'

Hannah tries to jiggle Megan the way Dad does when he's nursing her in the lounge room. *This is the way the ladies ride, hobbledy hoy, hobbledy hoy.* But Megan is heavy and she rolls sideways and falls on the floor and starts crying.

Mum comes down off the ladder. 'You have to be a bit more careful with her, Hannah. She probably needs changing.' She picks Megan up and takes her out of the room.

'I didn't drop her,' says Hannah. 'She just fell.'

'Don't worry about it,' says Dad. 'Babies are tough.'

They stop for afternoon tea. Lena and Sue have made a chocolate cake that is only a little bit soggy in the middle, and they serve it with a squirt of fake cream. Megan sucks crumbs and cream off Mum's fingers.

'Nearly finished,' says Dad.

'Good,' says Lena. 'That means Hannah gets out of our room.'

'It's not your room yet,' says Hannah. 'Not till I'm properly gone.' She takes a second serving of cake. 'And I'm going to take the tiger-cub posters and the one about the fireworks at the Opera House.'

'You can have them,' says Sue.

'And I want the computer, too.'

'You can't have that.'

'It's partly mine. You have to share.'

'But there's two of us and only one of you. It stays in our room.'

'There's two of us. Me. Megan.'

'Megan can't use a computer.'

'I'll teach her.'

'She's only a baby, stupid.'

Chapter Two
A Change in Plans

*H*annah is clearing the table. She gathers the empty glasses and balances them inside coffee mugs. She scrapes the last splashes of tomato sauce from her plate onto Mum's and then picks up Lena's.

'I'm not scraping this,' she says. 'She's hardly eaten it. She can scrape it herself.'

'You have to,' says Lena. 'It's your job.'

The doorbell rings.

'That'll be Amy,' says Dad. 'She's coming to babysit.'

'Why?' says Lena. 'Where are you going?'

'She's just going to look after you for an hour

or so while Mum and I go to the hospital to visit
Grandpa. We won't be long. You help her with
Megan.'

It takes a while for them to leave. Mum shows
Amy where the nappies are and the bottles of milk
in the fridge. She explains the way Megan likes to
be held when she drinks and then how she has to
be patted on the back and what to do if she cries.
Dad stays in the kitchen.

'We're not going till jobs are done,' he says.
Hannah scrapes and stacks. Sue washes. Lena dries.

Finally the door closes. Lena, Sue and Hannah
sit on the lounge room floor at Amy's feet. She is
cuddling Megan. Amy tucks her long red hair back
and Hannah sees she has four silver earrings. One
is a dolphin. Another a whale. There are wide silver
rings on her fingers.

'. . . *rings on her fingers and bells on her toes*
she shall have music wherever she goes . . .'

Hannah wants to ask Amy to take her shoes off so she can check, but Lena and Sue will laugh at her.

Amy tells the twins and Hannah what it is like being big and at high school. There are six different teachers for each class, and when the bell rings you have to go to a different room. Hannah only has one teacher, and he stays with them in the same room all day, except for library and PE. Sometimes he takes the class outside to do art or writing on the verandah, in the sunshine.

Gradually, as Amy talks, Megan falls asleep. Lena and Sue go off to play on the computer.

'Do you want to see my tomorrow room?' says Hannah.

Amy follows Hannah along the hall, around the corner where it turns past Mum and Dad's room and then on to the new doorway cut through the old back wall of the house. Hannah turns the light on. The ceiling glows like freshly spread margarine.

'Excellent,' says Amy. 'Who chose these cool colours?'

Hannah grins. 'I did. It's going to be the best room in the house.'

Amy promises to come and see it when Hannah has moved in her bed and her bookcase and the dolls' house made from fruit boxes.

'And is it all for you?' she says.

'And Megan,' says Hannah. 'But I chose everything. She's too little.' Hannah screws her nose up at the lingering smell of paint. 'I'm moving in tomorrow. Then it will be my today room.' She laughs and steps into the room and walks around it, stroking the window frame and each of the walls.

Hannah is reading when her parents get home. She hears them coming up the steps, talking in quick, urgent voices.

'Whatever you want,' Mum is saying. 'Whatever you think is right.'

What are they talking about? What does Dad think is right? Answers to maths homework are right. Correct spelling is right. Being right about punctuation means knowing when to put a question mark and when to put a full stop. Hannah jumps up and opens the door. Mum is holding Dad's hand. She drops it and gives Hannah a hug and holds on to her a bit more tightly than Hannah expects.

They chat to Amy, then pay her and watch while she goes out into the dark night, across the road to her house.

Dad calls Lena and Sue to come into the

kitchen. He has a *Come here, now* voice so they come and the whole family, except for Megan, sits at the table as if they are about to eat a meal.

'You tell them,' he says.

Mum rests the palms of her hands on the table and speaks slowly.

'You know Grandpa has been really sick . . .'

The girls look quickly from one to the other. 'Is he dead?' says Sue.

Mum shakes her head. 'No, but he's still unwell and he can't go home and look after himself. He can't stay in hospital, so Dad and I have been thinking that he should come here.'

Silence.

But there's no spare bed. There's no spare room. Guests sleep on the camping mattress on the lounge-room floor.

'Where's he going to sleep?' says Hannah. She is counting bedrooms. There is one room for Mum and Dad and there is the room she shares with her sisters.

And there is her new room.

Her tomorrow room.

A shiver runs from the back of her neck to her legs. She is cold and quivering.

'Not,' she whispers, 'not my room.'

Her father nods. 'I'm afraid so, Hannah. I know it will be hard for you. I know you were looking forward to it. But we don't have a choice. He is my father. He has no one else. He's a frail, old man.' He reaches across and pats Hannah's shoulder. She pulls away from him.

'Why can't he . . . why can't he . . .' She has nothing to suggest. There is nothing to say. She shrinks in her chair. She curls up and rolls off onto the floor. She gets up and heads down the hallway. Her mother moves as if to follow but changes her mind and stays at the table.

'It's hard for Hannah,' she says to Lena and Sue.

'Hard for us, you mean,' says Lena. 'We have to keep putting up with her when she . . .'

Hannah can't hear the rest. She has taken her blanket and pillow. When she reaches the door of her tomorrow room, she doesn't switch on the

light. She knows the ceiling glows with rich
yellow, the walls wrap around her with warm, blue
tones. She steps into the space that would be hers.
It's a space without twins, a space for her and
Megan. They were to move tomorrow. She
clutches the blanket tightly around her. She tries
to picture her grandfather but she cannot bring
his face into her mind.

Dad says he is frail. Frail means little and thin like you're going to fall down. Grandpa is tall, taller than Mum. Hannah remembers him when she was about four. He was burning leaves at the end of the yard. She wandered down to see him, past the budgie cages, the lemon tree and the spinach plants. He was standing over the tin drum. 'Stay back,' he shouted. 'Stay back.' But she didn't and a spark jumped and burnt her hand, and when he bent to help her she cried and ran away to Grandma who wrapped her hand in ice and held her close. Grandma is gone now. The scar is gone, too, but Hannah remembers where it was and lifts her hand to her mouth and kisses it better.

There's a splash of moonlight under the window. She puts her pillow there and drops down onto it, and when her parents find her she is fast asleep.

Chapter Three
School

Year Two has just had fitness. They have run around the oval twice and Hannah is the first one home. She is puffed, bent over and blowing hard. Her lungs hurt and her legs hurt but she has beaten Chris Martens and that is all she cares about. The bell goes for little lunch and she walks with Annie and Tui back to where their bags are, under the trees near the library steps.

Hannah has biscuits smeared with peanut butter. They are the kind of biscuits that have little holes all over them and when you squeeze two together, the peanut butter oozes out like burnt orange worms. She licks each biscuit clean. Tui has slices of watermelon, wrapped in plastic and Annie has homemade cake from her brother's birthday. It's an alien cake with green icing covered in red and blue spots. She doesn't like the taste of blue, and she picks a piece off and flicks it to the seagulls that flap and screech around the playground.

'When can we come and play in your new room?' Annie says.

Annie is an only child and has her own room but it is small and they know it well. The wardrobe is big and behind the door. The bed can only fit in the space under the window. The desk is up against the only spare wall. There can be no changes and no secrets in Annie's room.

Tui has always shared with her younger brother and sister. Her mum and dad have already added onto their house and there's no room for any more.

Hannah shakes her head. 'It's not my room, any more,' she says. She has finished her biscuits and licks the peanut butter from the tips of her fingers.

'My grandpa's sick and he's going to stay with us. He has to sleep there. Mum says when he's better I can have it back.'

'When will that be?' she'd asked her mother. They were in the kitchen. Mum was pulling the comb hard through Hannah's wet hair. There were lots of knots and the comb kept getting stuck and tugging so that Hannah cried out in pain.

'I don't know,' said Mum. 'Don't ask me.'

'Probably never,' said Sue.

Mum kept combing. Hannah bit her lip and stayed silent, even though tiny tears squeezed from her eyes like the last drops of honey from an empty jar. The thought of the tomorrow room without her was almost more than she could bear.

Annie is interested. 'Why doesn't he live at his house?'

'He's too sick.'

'Haven't you got a grandma who can look after him?'

'Not that one. He's my dad's father and that grandma died when I was in kindergarten.'

Hannah can't remember much about that grandmother. She and Grandpa lived down the Coast. There was that Christmas of the burnt hand and Grandma with the ice. There were peppermint lollies always kept in a cupboard that Hannah could reach. There are pictures of Grandma at Mum and Dad's wedding, dressed in mauve and sometimes if Hannah screws her eyes up tight the woman in the photograph moves inside her head like a memory. The dress is always the same and there is a white handbag over her shoulder no matter how Hannah's mind tries to place her.

'Is he going to be there for a long time?' says Tui.

Hannah shrugs. 'No one knows. Or maybe they know but they aren't telling me.'

Annie takes charge. 'Maybe you could get him to leave.'

'How?'

'Either you make him better and he goes home or . . .'

'I can't do that. I'm not a doctor or a nurse.'

'Or you make everything so horrible that he goes anyway. He doesn't want to stay.'

Hannah feels uncomfortable. She's never set out to be bad before. She doesn't know what to do.

'My grandma only stays a few days when she

comes to our place,' says Tui. 'She says we drive her mad 'cause we make too much noise and we leave our stuff everywhere and we want to watch television all the time. She fights with Mum about us and she says she goes back to her place for peace and quiet.'

Peace and quiet. Megan crying, Ceefer miaowing, Lena and Sue yelling at Hannah for being there when they want to be by themselves.

'I don't know,' says Hannah. 'I don't know what I'll do.'

Hannah walks up the hill, with Sue and Lena.

'Grandpa'll be there when we get home,' she says.

'Tell us about it.' Sue turns away.

'Means we keep you in our room,' says Lena.

'I don't like it any more than you do.'

Hannah wants to tell them that she's thinking of finding a way to make him leave, but they might say she's stupid and tell Mum and Dad and then there'll be trouble.

Hannah drops back. She kicks a clump of berries that are lying on the footpath. They skittle across the next driveway and land in the gutter.

She could scream and yell and run around crazily. She could turn the TV up and empty her schoolbag on the floor of the lounge room. She could act like a two-year-old and drive him bananas and maybe then he'd go. But Mum and Dad would stop her well before it got to that. They'd want to know what was going on. They'd take her aside and talk in soft, serious voices about how they knew she missed her room but look how sick Grandpa had been and how they all had to be considerate. And if she didn't answer, if she shrugged her shoulders and looked at the floor, they'd get angrier and tell her that she just had to stop, she was not to be selfish, she was to have some consideration and that was the end of it.

There are no more berries to kick so she bashes her bag against the paling fence in front of the corner house until it is covered in dusty white paint marks.

Chapter Four
Plan One

Mum meets them at the front door. She's rocking Megan in her arms and as the other girls walk up the path she puts a finger to her lips.

'Ssh. She's finally gone to sleep.' She follows them into the kitchen.

'And don't make a noise in the hallway. Grandpa's arrived and he's having a little lie down.'

Lena makes a show of moving from the fridge to the sink on her tip-toes. She tries ballet steps, spins around, slips and falls against the stove. The plastic jug flies out of her hands and bounces across the kitchen floor. Ceefer, showered with iced water, howls and dives for the back door.

Megan's eyes spring open and she cries, loudly.

'Thanks a lot,' hisses Mum as she retreats to the lounge room.

Hannah takes a mandarin and goes to dump her schoolbag near her bed. Her books and toys are in boxes ready for the move that isn't going to happen. Her half of the shelf space is bare. She is supposed to unpack everything this afternoon.

'Put it all back where it was,' Dad had said when he'd come to listen to her read last night. He'd lifted the framed photographs off the top of the pile. Hannah in her school uniform in Year One. She is smiling with her mouth determinedly closed to hide the gaps where her teeth are missing. Then there is one of Hannah and Megan taken in the hospital when Megan was only an hour old. The red-faced baby, wrapped tightly in hospital blankets, looks up at Hannah with huge dark eyes. Dad had put the photos on the top shelf of the bookcase, where they had always been. When he'd left the room, Hannah had taken them down and put them back in the packing case.

Now, she leaves the room and goes quietly along the hallway to the door of the tomorrow room. It is closed. There is no keyhole to spy through. She listens and thinks she hears someone breathing on the other side, but she cannot be sure. She wanders

back past the open door of her parents' room.
Mum is pacing up and down, patting Megan and
singing a song that Hannah doesn't understand.
When Hannah stops in the doorway and looks in
as if she is going to speak, Mum frowns and shakes
her head and waves Hannah away.

She goes via the kitchen and gets a drink and
makes a bowl of muesli. She goes outside and
down to the back wall of the house where there is
a window of the tomorrow room. It is too high off
the ground for her to see in, even when she stands
on the mound of dirt and broken concrete left
after the building. She puts down the things she is
carrying and gets the wheelbarrow from the back
shed. There are spiders under the handles and a
small, rusty hole in the bottom. She wheels the
barrow under the window, balances herself
carefully on either side of the hole and pulls herself
up to the sill.

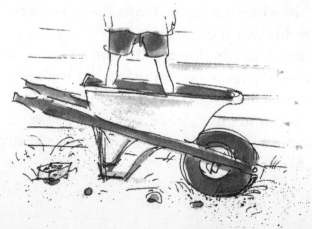

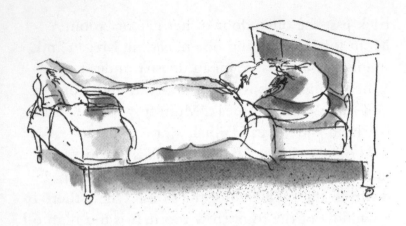

Grandpa is lying on his back, mouth open,
asleep. He is covered in a sheet but one leg sticks
out. His thin ankle pokes from the bottom of his
striped pyjamas. The room is almost bare. His
suitcase, open, lies on the floor beside the upturned
toybox that is covered in bottles of tablets, a glass
of water, a small grey box and his glasses. As
Hannah watches, he stirs, coughs, turns over and
his thin white hair floats across the pale green
pillow like wisps of spiderweb.

Hannah climbs down and wanders up to her
space between the jacaranda and the back fence.
She squats in the dirt and eats her muesli.

Get him to leave, Annie said. Easy to say.

Ceefer comes and rubs herself against Hannah's
legs. She pulls her ears.

'I wish Grandpa was allergic to you. Then I'd put you in his bed and he'd get itchy and then he'd go.'

Ceefer purrs.

Hannah picks a yellow dandelion and tugs each petal from the centre. 'He goes. He stays. He goes. He stays. He goes. He stays. He goes.'

But how? She wraps her arms around her knees and drops her chin forward.

A snail has crawled onto her shoelace. It is almost up to her shoe. She looks back along the silver trail. Three others are crawling along an outer stem of a pink impatiens. They have stripped it of leaves.

Snails. Snails in his shoes. Snails in his socks. Snails in his slippers. Slippery, squelchy snails between the toes.

Hannah goes to the garden shed and finds an old seedling container. She lines it with leaves and handfuls of grass. Then she pulls the snails from the stem and drops them on top of the greenery.

'Hannah,' Mum calls from the back door. 'I'm just going down to the shop for some bread. Megan's asleep and the twins are on the computer. Don't disturb your grandfather.'

Hannah tiptoes through the house. She can hear the zapping sounds of a computer game from her room. There's silence from Mum and Dad's room. At the door of the tomorrow room, she stops. What if he's awake? Look, Grandpa. Look what I've brought to show you. She turns the handle and pushes the door slightly. No sound.

Her grandfather has rolled onto his back again, sleeping, mouth open. His hands, as pale as rice-paper, lie folded across his chest. It rattles as he breathes. His slippers lie at the foot of the bed. Hannah creeps towards them. She kneels and lifts the snails and one by one pushes them as far into the toes of his slippers as she can.

A snorting sound comes from the bed. The mattress creaks as the old man turns and lies on his side, facing into the room. Hannah holds her breath. All is quiet again. She backs silently from the room.

Hannah is sitting at the kitchen table, copying her spelling words from the sheet into her book. Dad is slicing onions for a vegetable stir-fry. Hannah has just covered the word 'laugh' and is trying to remember which letter comes first, the *a* or the *u,* when her grandfather comes slowly into the room. His dressing-gown is loose around his shoulders. He leans against the door frame and then the kitchen bench. He is wearing one of his slippers, the other is in his hand. He drops heavily into the chair opposite Hannah and reaches his hand into the slipper, into the space for his toes. She wants to look away but cannot. Her grandfather draws the snails out one by one and puts them on the newspaper that Dad has been reading. They start to leave a silvery trail across the face of the Prime Minister.

'Funny things, snails,' says Grandpa. 'Some people think they're really slimy and disgusting. When I was in France in the war, I got a real taste for them.' He looks across at Hannah. 'French people love the taste of snails. And frogs' legs. They cook them with lots of oil and garlic and they serve them with parsley and – '

Dad turns from the bench. 'Are you offering those to me to cook?'

Grandpa winks across the table. 'Only if Hannah will join me.'

Chapter Five
Plan Two

Dinner is finished. Television is banned because
Lena left her mug of chocolate milk on the
lounge-room floor and Ceefer knocked it over.
White cat hairs float on the brown stains seeping
between the floorboards.

Hannah and Megan are alone in the lounge
room. Hannah arranges a stand over Megan's
bouncinette. Hanging from it are coloured cloth
balls and squeaky toys, pieces of ribbon and two
old spoons.

Megan reaches out and swipes the balls.

'Good girl,' says Hannah and she flicks the spoons
against each other so they clang. Megan grins.

Hannah squeezes the plastic monkey that hangs by its tail. It whistles and squeaks.

Megan's grin widens. Two tiny white teeth are pushing their way through her bottom gum. She gurgles and dribbles. Hannah pushes the wire frame of the bouncinette, up and down. Up and down. Megan giggles, dribbles and laughs. She kicks her legs. Hannah bounces her higher and higher.

'Stop it. Hannah, what are you doing?' Mum comes into the room and crouches to steady Megan.

'She likes that.'

'Maybe. But she's just been fed. She'll be sick.'

'But she was laughing.'

'You're the one who'll be laughing when she throws up everything and you have to clean it up.' Mum lifts Megan onto her shoulder and pats her softly on the back. 'There, there. Settle down.'

Hannah stands up. 'I can't do anything around here.' She kicks the bouncinette against a chair and slams the door behind her.

Her father finds her, sitting on her bed, facing the wall.

'Time for a story?'

There is a tiny crack in the plaster. Hannah

wedges her fingernail into it and scratches to make it as large as she can. She doesn't answer him.

He sits down beside her and puts his hand on her arm. 'Stop that, Hannah. You're wrecking the wall.'

'Good. No one cares about me. Why should I care about an old wall?'

'We do care about you. We care an enormous amount about you. We also care about your grandfather and your sisters and the whole family and we're all caught up in this situation.'

'Well, you don't show it.'

'What do you want, Hannah?'

'I want him to get out of my room. I want him to give it back.'

'That's impossible, and you know it.'

'He's not so sick that he has to stay in bed. He walked out to the kitchen without even a walking stick. Why can't he go and live somewhere else? Why does he have to live with us?'

'Because we live in Sydney near the hospital. Because he's been really sick and needs care. And even though he can get around a bit he's still not really well. Because he's our father and grandfather and we love him and want to take care of him.'

'Well I don't.'

'I think that's enough, Hannah. I think you should go to bed and think how you'd feel if you were in Grandpa's shoes right now.'

He leaves the room.

Hannah drops on the pillow. In Grandpa's shoes? What about his slippers? Still sticky with the silver snail slime. What about his black shoes, under the bed? Big black shoes. She could put her feet in them and charge across the room. Flip flop. Slip slop. She giggles and turns to face the wall, pulling a blanket up tightly over her shoulders.

On Sunday evening, Hannah is in the bedroom with all the bits of her construction set spread out on the floor. She is building a house, a huge rambling house with long hallways and rooms that lead into other rooms. Bedrooms and sitting rooms, television rooms and playing rooms, rooms to eat in and rooms to do nothing in. Happy rooms, sad rooms and angry rooms. They stretch from the end of her bed to the bookcase under the window. She has a box of tiny plastic people and she takes each one and places it in a separate space, telling them quietly where they are and what they can do.

Sue comes in and flops on the lower bunk.

'What's that smell?' she says.

'What smell?'

'There's something off around here.'

'It's not me.'

Hannah adds another room to her house, a room to argue in.

'Well it's something,' says Sue and she rolls off the bed and peers under the wardrobe. She sniffs like a tracker dog. 'Not here.' She pokes her nose into the crack between the wall and the bookcase. Sniff. Sniff. She crawls to where Hannah is building. Sniff. 'Is it a stinking toilet you've got here?'

'Clear off.'

Sue looks under Hannah's bed.

'Ah huh.' She pulls out Hannah's sports bag.
'I bet it's this.' She tips up the bag and out fall
shorts, a swimming costume, a damp towel
speckled with black mould, dirty socks, lolly
wrappers, two apple-cores, broken goggles and
something else. It's square-shaped, half wrapped
in clear plastic. The edges are green, the light green
of freshly mown grass. Seeping from the dark
green centre is a streak of orange, tinged with the
brown of burnt saucepans.

'What's that?' Sue sits back and pushes it over
with the corner of a book. Two big cockroaches
crawl out from underneath.

'I don't know.'

'I think, in another life, it was a peanut-butter
sandwich.'

The smells hit Hannah. She pulls away from the pile on the floor. Her stomach churns. She swallows hard. She wants to vomit. She cannot jump up and run while Sue is watching.

'Yuck! You're disgusting,' says Sue. 'You are putrid, you are sick-making. No one can live in a room with that stuff. Get it out of here.' She goes off down the hall, calling, 'Mum, Mum, Hannah's being revolting.'

Hannah opens the window and takes a huge breath. She turns back to the pile of smells on the floor. She picks up a tennis racquet, shoves everything back into the bag and zips it up. Then she tosses it out the window.

When Sue comes back into the room with
Lena, Hannah is on the floor calmly adding a
room to the house. A smelly room.

Hannah takes no notice of her sisters. She has
turned her back and she hears them giggling and
plotting.

'Do you want to see what we're doing?' says
Sue.

'No.'

'You will when you know what it is.'

Hannah stares firmly at her little plastic people.
They are squat, solid and square. They don't move
unless she makes them. They don't talk unless she
speaks for them and they do not argue with each
other.

The laughing continues. Hannah moves her
head slightly and looks out of the corner of her
eye. She cannot see what they are doing. She lets
a building piece drop and it rolls towards the
bookcase. She reaches for it, glances sideways and
sees her sisters sitting on the bottom bunk tying
shoelaces together to make a long thin rope.

Sue stands above her. 'See this,' she says. 'This is
to make a line down the middle.' She drops one
end at the bookcase and walks across the room to
the far wall. 'What's on that side is yours. A third of
the bookcase and a third of the wardrobe and a

third of the room. You aren't allowed to come over on our side. Don't you even put your foot over on this side. Not even your big toe. Not even your little finger.'

Hannah looks from the bookcase, around the room to the bunks and then the wardrobe and then around to her own bed. 'Suits me,' she says. 'I don't want to go in your stupid section. But the same goes for you. Don't you step in my section either.'

Lena and Sue are laughing. 'She hasn't noticed,' says Sue.

'She will when she gets hungry,' says Lena.

'Or when she has to go to the loo.'

Hannah is confused.

Sue stands up and goes over to the door. She closes it and folds her arms and leans back casually against it like someone in a big crime movie, showing a prisoner how they are trapped.

'This is in our territory. You can't use it.'

Hannah shrugs. 'I don't care. I'll just go in and out the window.' She leaves her game and climbs up onto the bookcase and sits on the window sill. It's dark outside. Light from her tomorrow room falls across the yard. Her sports bag lies where it has fallen, upside-down in the space under the lemon ti-tree. What was it Sue said? *No one can live in a room with that stuff.* No one? Not even a grandpa?

Hannah drops down from the window onto the grass. She finds a stick and hooks it under the strap of the bag and carries it carefully to the back door. She goes into the laundry and puts the bag down while she checks the kitchen and the hallway. She hears Mum singing to Megan in her room. She hears the television going in the lounge room and peeps through a crack in the doorway. Dad is watching the news. Grandpa is in the big chair next to the piano. His eyes are closed and his head hangs forward. As Hannah watches, he jerks, shakes himself awake and stares wide-eyed at the flickering screen.

All clear. Hannah picks up the bag and goes down to the tomorrow room. She pushes the door open. The light is on and she quickly opens the zip and slides the bag under the bed, at the head end.

Chapter Six
Cornered

Grandpa isn't at breakfast. Hannah writes her name in dribbles of honey that fall from her knife to her piece of toast.

'Go easy, Hannah. You don't need that much.' Dad is sipping his second cup of coffee. 'Martha, is the nurse coming today?'

Hannah is up to the last *h*. All the letters are running into each other.

'At nine o'clock,' says Mum. She's feeding Megan in the next room.

Nurse? What nurse?

'D'you need a hand?' He gets up to rinse his cup.

A hand? What for?

'No. Everything's under control.'

Her mother puts Megan up on her shoulder and pats her back. Milk dribbles over her chin and down onto the stained purple dressing gown.

'What are you two talking about,' says Hannah.

'The community nurse,' says Dad. She's coming to shower Grandpa.'

'Can't he shower himself?' Hannah screws up her face. She's been bathing herself since she was three.

Dad shakes his head. 'I don't think you realise how sick he's been, Hannah. If he was in the shower by himself, he could have a fall and not be able to get up again. He's on all sorts of drugs for his heart problems and for blood pressure and other things as well. They do funny things to your system.'

'Like what?' She bites into her toast. It is so sweet.

'Well, his balance is a bit affected. He gets giddy sometimes and his senses of smell and taste have gone. You might have noticed, he's not eating very much.'

His sense of smell.

'Yuk,' says Hannah.

'So if he's going to stay here for a while,

we need help in looking after him. The nurse will get him out of bed, showered, dressed. That sort of thing.'

So the nurse will go into his room.

'What's up, Hannah?'

Hannah rubs her tummy. 'I've got a bit of a pain. I think I'd better go to the toilet.' She gets down from the table and goes quickly along the hallway to her tomorrow room. He won't have smelt a thing. If the nurse finds it? If Mum does? Or Dad?

The door is ajar. She hesitates. He's still asleep, face to the wall. Hannah drops to her knees and crawls forward. She feels under the bed. Slippers. A tissue. A coin. The strap of her bag.

The smell reaches out to her. It curls around the inside of her throat. Damp smell. Rotting smell. She swallows hard.

Footsteps come along the hall. Mum's voice. 'I'll just pop in and see if he's awake.'

'I'll do it.'

That's Dad. Two lots of footsteps. Hannah dives under the bed. The footsteps are at the door.

The smell clutches her stomach, squeezes her chest.

'There's something off in here.' Mum whispers.

'Yeah. It's a bit rank.'

Hannah hears the window open.

'Where exactly is it coming from?'

'Dunno.' Dad moves closer to the bed. 'You don't think . . . ?'

'What?'

'He might've had an accident in the night. You know. Not made it to the toilet.'

'I don't think so. It's not quite that smell. It's more like something rotten.' They are whispering urgently. Hannah can barely hear them. Her face is pressed to the floor. Her nose is only an arm's length from the bag. She thinks she's going to vomit. She feels the honey and the milk and the cereal from breakfast rising in her chest. It reaches her throat. She stuffs her fist into her mouth.

'We'll have to find out what it is,' her mother whispers. 'The nurse'll be here soon.'

Hannah's eyes are closed. Don't look under the bed. Don't. Her eyes are fixed on the soft, brown leather of her father's shoes. Then the blue denim of his jeans as he drops to his knees.

Any minute he'll find her. What will she say? I smelt the smell and I was worried about Grandpa so I came in to look for it. I didn't want to wake him so I crept in quietly and thought I'd look under the bed.

Dad's hands come into view and then the bottom of his beard. Hannah has a sudden desire to pull it, but she doesn't dare take her fist from her mouth.

'I think I'm getting warmer. It pongs down here.' His face comes into view. Eyes widen. He hisses, 'Hannah! What in the blazes are you doing here?'

Chapter Seven
Plan Three

'**G**et out!' Dad speaks slowly, deliberately. It's a *don't argue with me* voice. 'Just get out and take that putrid bag with you.'

Hannah wriggles forward, one foot hooked into the bag strap so it follows her like a faithful dog. Mum wrinkles her nose.

'Oh, Hannah,' she says.

The bag trails Hannah along the hallway and through the kitchen to the back door. Lena and Sue look up from making their lunches.

'Poo. You stink,' says Lena.

Sue makes gagging noises.

Hannah stands on the back step, picks up the

bag and hurls it as far as she can. Dirty socks, mouldy towel and green sandwich lie scattered on the grass.

'I just don't understand, Hannah,' says Dad. He has followed her and stands on the verandah looking down at her. 'I know you're disappointed in not getting the room, but you can't always get what you want in life. You know that and you know that Grandpa is sick and old and he's only got us to take care of him. It's as if you're trying to drive him away.'

Hannah says nothing. Ceefer climbs lazily out of the wheelbarrow and walks slowly across the lawn. She stalks the green sandwich, her body pressed low to the ground, ears alert and twitching.

'We don't want to have any more of this nonsense, all right?' says Dad.

Still she says nothing. Ceefer has stretched out a paw and is playing with the mouldy bread. She cuffs it, flicks it over and dances around it.

Dad goes inside. Hannah stays for a moment and then goes back in and brushes past her mother and sisters in the kitchen. In the lounge room, Megan is lying on a rug on the floor. Hannah drops down beside her and puts her arm across the baby's tummy. Megan gurgles and flings her arms out, laughing. Hannah kneels and her hair falls over Megan's face. Tiny hands grab at the hair. Hannah rubs her nose against Megan's belly and her little sister squeals with such delight that Hannah laughs too and rolls back onto the floor, holding Megan above her.

At little lunch, Hannah walks round and round the oval with Annie and Tui. She tries not to look at Sue and Lena who are playing soccer in the middle of the field.

'It doesn't work,' she says. 'I tried to scare him off. Either he loves what I've been doing or he doesn't even know I've done it.'

'Put a sheet over you and be a ghost,' says Tui. 'Let him think the house is haunted.'

'Don't be hopeless.' Hannah shakes her head. 'He doesn't believe in ghosts. I don't believe in ghosts. If he hasn't got his glasses on he won't even see me and even if he does he won't hear properly.'

The bell rings and a ball from the soccer game

flies across the field and whacks her on the knee. She falls in a crumpled heap.

Hannah and Annie are in the library for research on endangered species. They are looking in a book about rainforest creatures.

'He needs a wife,' says Annie.

'Who?' says Hannah. 'Him?' She points to the three-toed sloth hanging upside-down from a branch.

'Your grandfather, stupid.'

'I'm not stupid,' says Hannah. 'I knew that's who you meant.' She stares at the picture. If he had a wife, they wouldn't fit in her room. They wouldn't want to stay in the house. They'd need a house for themselves.

'I don't know where you get one. They don't have shops or catalogues for that sort of thing. I don't know any old women except my other grandmother and she's already got a husband, and my nanna, she's my great-grandmother and she stays in bed all day.

'You can advertise,' says Annie. 'My mum knows someone who found a husband that way. You just put it in the paper.'

'Put what in the paper?' Mr Martin, the librarian stands behind Hannah.

'Nothing, sir,' says Annie.

'Come on. It must have been important if you were discussing it instead of working.'

Hannah pauses. 'A lost cat, sir,' she says, in a rush, and she sees again Ceefer curiously tossing the sandwich, dancing with it in and out of the dandelions. 'I lost my cat and Annie said we could advertise and put it in the paper.'

'Very sensible,' says Mr Martin. 'But it's not an endangered species and so you will not waste your precious time worrying about it in my lesson.'

He goes back to where Chris Martens and Mark are playing marbles in the reading pit.

After school, Annie and Tui come to play. They rescue all the newspapers from the recycling box and spread them over the back verandah. They flick through the pages of politicians, sporting stars and cartoons that they don't understand. Mum comes out to give them chopped up oranges and the funny squashed-looking biscuits with chocolate sprinkles that Lena made.

'What are you looking for?' she asks.

'Just ads,' says Hannah. 'For a special project.'

'What sort of ads? Things for sale?'

'Not exactly.' How can Hannah explain? We need an ad for someone who wants a husband?

'Well, do you mean job ads? Small businesses? People who'll come and lop your tree, fix your broken pipes or clear away stuff you don't want?'

'That's more like it,' says Hannah.

'You want the local paper.' Mum picks it up and turns to the back pages.

'Mm. Here we are. *General Classifieds*, *Health and Beauty*, *Meeting People*, you don't want that. That's for people looking for partners. *All Trades*. This is it.' She drops the paper in front of Hannah and goes back inside.

People looking for Partners. Hannah grabs the page and reads to the others.

'*Lady 45, non-smoker, seeks gentleman, 45–55 . . .*

That's no good. Grandpa's nearly eighty. *Zany,*
outgoing lady. Own home. Seeks companion for travel,
theatre visits, fun runs, the gym.'

'That would keep him busy,' says Tui.

'I don't think he could go on a fun run.'

Annie peers over Hannah's shoulder. 'This looks
like a good one, *Highly educated, caring woman* –
That's what you want – *seeks friendship with polite,*
sensitive man. Is he polite?' Hannah nods. 'Except he
falls asleep when he's watching television.' '*Must be*
fit, healthy and attractive.'

Hannah drops the paper. 'It's no good. None
of these people want him. We'll just have to write
our own.'

'Hannah!' Mum calls from the kitchen. 'Hannah.'

Hannah goes inside. Mum holds out a cup of
tea with a biscuit resting on the saucer. 'Take this
in to Grandpa. He's in the lounge room.'

Hannah doesn't want to but she doesn't know
how to say no.

Grandpa is sitting on the edge of the heavy
green lounge chair.

The small grey box from his bedside table is on
the floor. He has a glass ball in his hand and he's
shaking it and holding it out to Megan in the
bouncinette. She reaches up as his hand steadies
and the tiny white flakes inside the glass dome

settle over a miniature Harbour Bridge.

'Look, Hannah,' says Grandpa. 'Look how she loves this. Megan the Pegan.' He shakes the dome again and, without turning to Hannah, says, 'I used to call you Hannah-Goanna when you were this age.'

Hannah wants to reach out. She wants to kneel beside Megan and stretch out and hold the dome and shake it and watch the flurry falling and the Bridge emerge.

'Here's your tea,' she says. 'And everyone knows it never snows in Sydney.'

Chapter Eight
The Advertisement

*T*ui and Annie are waiting for her when she comes back to the verandah. They look to Hannah to write the ad. She knows her grandfather. She'll have the words to write about him. Ceefer comes lazily across the lawn. She arches her neck and rubs her soft furry back against Hannah's leg.

Hannah picks up the paper again. She could forget about the ad. She could take the girls in now and they could play with Megan. Tickle her and bounce her on their knees. Kneel over her and move her arms and legs, teaching her to crawl. They could shake the snowdome and watch her laugh and reach out as the tiny flakes fall.

'What do other ads say?'

'Anybody out there? Adventurous male seeks energetic companion.'

'No. That's not quite right.' Hannah reads another one.

'My friends say I'm good looking. You may agree . . .'

'Sounds up himself.'

'Handsome professional man seeks slim attractive lady.'

'None of them are any good.'

'Be honest,' says Tui. 'Say what you really want.'

'Sure thing,' says Hannah. 'Sick old man seeks wife to look after him and stop him from living in granddaughter's bedroom.'

They are quiet again.

The afternoon sun goes behind a cloud. Hannah feels her words have gone, too.

'You could call him, *"elderly gentleman"*,' Tui says. She's skimming the list of ads in the paper. 'And then you put his hobbies and then you say, *"seeks lady with similar interests"*.'

'What are his hobbies?' says Annie.

'Sleeping in front of the TV,' says Hannah. She's trying to remember what he did before he got sick. At his house, two Christmases ago, she helped him pick hydrangeas. He had bushes all along the fence and he lifted her up and she worked the secateurs to cut the stalks. Pale pink, sky blue and deep mauve, the heads were huge. Hannah, loaded down with bunches and bunches raced back to the house and filled vase after vase, coffee jars and empty containers of peanut butter and honey. 'They were your grandmother's favourites,' he'd said. But Grandma wasn't there any more.

'Gardening,' she says. 'And he used to play the trumpet in the town band when Dad was little. So we can put down music.'

'OK. How about this,' says Tui. *'Elderly gent, keen gardener and music lover, seeks lady with similar interests.'*

Hannah writes the words in the space provided at the bottom of the page. She hesitates when she gets to the last line. *Signature.* She cannot sign his name. She doesn't know what it looks like.

'Neither do they,' says Annie. 'Just practise for a bit on the edge of the paper and then do it.' Hannah scribbles *Arthur Taylor, Arthur Taylor, Arthur Taylor* around the edges of the newspaper. Finally she signs on the dotted line, a sweeping signature with a flourishing, curly tail at the end of each word.

'Good,' says Annie. 'Someone can answer that and then he can get married and you can be the flower-girl and bring us a bit of the cake.'

They finish their biscuits. Tui has the scissors. She is about to cut the ad out of the paper when she reads through the print.

'We can't do this. Look.' She points to the space at the bottom. 'You have to pay. You need a credit-card number.'

'I haven't got a credit card.'

'Or a cheque.'

'I haven't got a cheque.'

The flower-girl fades from Hannah's mind. The tomorrow room, her room, fades too.

'Hang on,' says Annie. 'When we wanted to get rid of our puppies, we put a sign up at the supermarket. There's a board there.'

'Did you have to pay?'

'I don't think so. We just wrote it out and Mum stuck it up when she went to do the shopping.'

'Did it work?'

Tui nodded. 'It's the only way, Hannah. I can put it up. We're going there tonight.'

A fresh sheet of paper is found. Hannah copies the ad in her best writing. She puts the address and phone number on in big printing. The flower-girl creeps back into her mind.

Tui puts the sheet in her pocket.

Elderly gent, keen
gardener and music lover,
Seeks lady with
Similar interests.
POPLAR GROVE,
PETERSHAM
PH: 9672415

Dinner is finished and it's Hannah's turn to clear the table.

Grandpa has had his meal in front of the television in the lounge room and now he seems to have fallen asleep. She goes to get his plate. He hasn't touched the slices of chicken. The potato salad and the other vegetables have been half eaten. There's a splash of the peanut sauce that Dad made on his chin and two green beans have dropped onto his chest.

Hannah picks up the plate and hesitates. Mum and Dad have followed her and are standing in the doorway.

'He's not eating,' whispers Mum. 'He'll never get better like this.'

'Maybe old-fashioned mashed vegies,' says Dad. 'Maybe that's what he wants.'

'Maybe he's not hungry.' Hannah bends down and picks the beans off her grandfather's shirt.

'Ta, love.' He doesn't open his eyes.

Chapter Nine
Assembly Item

'**D**id you put it up on the board?' Hannah is standing next to Tui in lines.

Tui nods. 'When Mum went to the butcher, I said I had to get a book for a project and she let me go to the supermarket by myself. I stuck it next to one about community shopping help for old people. I thought they might read it.'

Hannah nods slowly. She pictures that sheet of white paper on the noticeboard next to notes about lost dogs and babysitting and kids' old toys for sale.

'Good one,' says Annie and she links her arm through Tui's and pushes ahead of Hannah as the class moves towards their room.

Year Two is practising their item for Assembly. They have made flags from all the countries that their families have come from and they are going to hold them as they sing 'I am Australian'.

Hannah is sitting between Mark and Valerie. Mark is holding the Portuguese flag. Valerie holds the Aboriginal flag. Hannah didn't know whether to make a flag from New Zealand, for Dad's parents or one from Ireland for Mum's great-grandparents. Then Dad told the story of one of his great-grandmothers who came from Finland, so Hannah painted a big blue cross on a white background.

The practice finishes and Mrs Marsden lines the class up at the door. Hannah and Mark are the leaders.

'Hold hands with your partner,' says Mrs Marsden.

Hannah has never held Mark's hand. She doesn't want to hold it now. She holds her flag with both hands and looks down at her feet.

'I said holding hands, everyone.' Mrs Marsden pushes between the children and the door. She has been conducting the class energetically and there are big dark sweat circles under her arms.

Hannah stares at them.

Mark grabs Hannah's hand. Hannah pulls it away. Mark grabs it again.

'Don't you want to be the leader, Hannah?'

'Yes, Miss.' Hannah leaves her hand in Mark's damp clutch.

'Excellent,' says Mrs MacIntosh, the principal, when they have finished their performance in the hall. 'You make me very proud of you.' She leads the whole school clapping. Hannah is smiling almost to bursting. Then she remembers, she must walk back with Mark.

They are almost to the door of the classroom when Chris Martens hisses from a few rows back. Hannah can't hear exactly what is said but she hears everyone laughing.

'What did he say?' she whispers to Annie who is behind her.

'He says that you're Mark's girlfriend,' Annie laughs.

Hannah wrenches her hand free. 'I am not.'

'Mark's girlfriend.' Hannah hears the whisper again.

'No way,' says Mark. 'She's ugly.'

Tears burn behind Hannah's eyes. She's not Mark's girlfriend. She doesn't even want to hold his hand. But she doesn't want to hear him say that.

'She wouldn't be my girlfriend,' says Mark, again. 'I wouldn't want her.'

Wouldn't want her. Wouldn't want her. The words buzz in Hannah's brain. They buzz all through the time for writing reports on the endangered species. They buzz through quiet time, packing up at the end of the day. They are still buzzing when Hannah runs to catch up with the twins at the gate at bell time.

'Your item wasn't bad,' says Sue. 'Better than the dance that kindergarten did. They couldn't even remember which way to go.'

Hannah isn't listening. She wants to go to the shopping centre and take down the note. She wants her room back. But she cannot leave the note there.

'We have to go shopping,' she says to her

mother as soon as they get in the door.

'Shh,' says Mum. 'Megan's just gone off to sleep. Whatever it is can wait.'

'We have to go shopping,' she says again when Megan wakes up and is having her nappy changed.

'No way,' says Mum. 'I've got another load of washing to do and I don't want to go out.'

'We really have to go shopping,' Hannah is almost crying as she hands her mother the pegs at the clothesline.

'Hannah, am I right in thinking something weird is going on? Why do we have to go shopping? Do you have something that you have to get?'

'A book for school.'

'It can wait till the weekend.'

'I need it tomorrow.'

'I'll write a note to the teacher.'

'I really, really need it. I'll get into big trouble.'

'I said I'll write a note.'

'She'll kill me.'

'Don't be dramatic, Hannah. Nothing's ever that bad.'

Chapter Ten
The Phone Calls

Spaghetti bolognese. Friday nights when everyone is tired and no one wants to cook. Sue takes a container of sauce out of the freezer and Lena puts a pot of water on the stove. They are the cooks for the night and Hannah has to help.

'Set the table,' says Sue.

'Fill the water jug,' says Lena.

'Find the cheese grater.'

Hannah does as she is told and then stands in the middle of the room, tired of their orders. Fast music comes on the radio. Lena claps while Sue grabs Hannah's hand and spins her around.

'Dance,' Sue says and spins herself, faster and

faster. Hannah joins her, madly twirling till laughing they stagger from the bench to a chair to the edge of the table.

Megan cheers and bangs a spoon on the tray of her high chair and spits out a soggy crust of bread.

Hannah is slurping long strands of spaghetti when the phone rings. Her father gets up to answer it.

'Pardon?' He screws up his face and shrugs his shoulders at the family around the table. 'No. I am not an elderly gentleman with a beautiful garden and musical interests.' He hangs up. 'Some weirdo.' He slides back into his seat. 'Obviously a wrong number.'

Hannah stares at her plate. She hadn't thought about who would answer the phone. Grandpa is lying down. He hasn't eaten dinner for the second night in a row and Mum has said not to disturb him.

The phone rings again. Hannah leaps up and her chair topples back against the fridge. Dad is quicker.

'Yes,' he says, 'this is 9672 415.' He is listening intently. 'No, I am not an elderly gentleman.' He slams the phone down.

'You are pretty old, Dad,' says Lena.

'Thanks a lot.' He mops his bolognese sauce

with a crust of bread. Megan bangs her spoon
again and bits of tomato fly across the table. Her
father picks them off his sleeve and from the front
of his shirt. '*You* don't think I'm ancient, do you,
Ginger Meggs?'

She grins. There is a rim of rich tomato sauce
around her mouth. Meat and pasta decorate her
bib, her hair, her pyjamas and chair.

'You need another bath,' he coos at her.

She grins and flicks the spoon at him. This time
the sauce lands in his eye.

Hannah is doing her
homework when the
phone rings for the
third time.

*What are three
celebrations in your family?*
is the question she has to
answer. She has written
Christmas and birthdays
and she is not sure what
else to write. Tui has
Moon Festival and
Chinese New Year.
Caterina has a name day
as well as a birthday.

Hannah would like a name day, too. Or a Moon Festival. Or a Sun Festival. Most of all she would like a Festival of the Tomorrow Room.

'Yes,' her father is saying into the phone. 'That's this number. No. I don't know what all this is about. What advertisement?'

Hannah looks up at him. Little lines gather at the corners of his lips, pressed tightly together. He reaches for a pen and scribbles something on the back of an envelope that is lying on the table.

He puts the phone down. 'Martha,' he calls. 'Lena. Sue.'

They gather around the table. Dad stays standing, his hands gripping the back of the chair.

'I don't really know what to do,' he says. 'I have just had the most amazing series of phone calls. Three of them, in fact.'

Ceefer slinks into the room. She arches her back and rubs up against Hannah's legs. Hannah wants to pick her up and take her outside. And stay there.

'Someone, and I'm not sure who, has put an ad on the noticeboard at the supermarket, looking for a . . . a woman, a wife for your grandfather.'

'A what?' Lena pulls a face.

Mum starts to giggle.

Dad frowns. 'Now then, Lena, Sue, Hannah?

It wouldn't be any of you, by any chance, would it?'

'No.' Lena and Sue look at Hannah.

Dad looks at Hannah.

Mum looks at Hannah.

Hannah looks down at the soft honey-coloured fur of Ceefer. She will never be Grandpa's flower-girl now.

'Hannah,' says Mum, 'is that what you were doing with the girls the other afternoon?'

Hannah nods.

Dad is striding around the kitchen. 'I have never been more embarrassed in my life. What were you thinking about, Hannah?'

Tears push in behind Hannah's eyes.

'I thought we made it perfectly clear that this business with your grandfather had to stop. It's unforgivable. Unthinkable. That a child of mine could treat my father . . .'

Hannah cannot look up. On the floor under the table there is a piece of sticky, yellow paper that Mum uses for phone messages. It is the same yellow as the ceiling in the tomorrow room. Not the tomorrow room. The next-year room, or the one after that. The never room. Never, never.

Mum looks at Lena and Sue. 'You two girls go off to bed. Dad and I want to talk to Hannah.'

'No,' says Dad. 'I'm far too angry to talk now. Go to bed, the lot of you. We'll talk about this tomorrow.'

'You're so stupid, Hannah,' says Lena. 'How did you think you'd get away with it? They'd know it was you.'

'Pretty sexist,' says Sue. 'Thinking you could get a woman to look after him. Pity it didn't work. You'd get your room back and we'd get some privacy.'

Hannah is last out of the bathroom. She's thirsty and tiptoes back along the hall to the kitchen. The door is closed. On the other side, from Mum and Dad, comes a strange, weird noise. Stifled laughter. Giggling that's deep down, that you don't want to burst out so you keep your mouth shut and even jam your fist in but some bits seep out anyway, like water in the pasta saucepan when the flame is up too high.

Footsteps cross the room. Hannah doesn't want to go to bed, but she doesn't want to be found, either. She starts to back away but the door doesn't open. She hears water run into the kettle, the flick of the gas lighter, the sound of cups being taken from the cupboard and placed on the bench. They are making tea and all the time talking in soft, low voices, broken every now and then by snatches of laughter.

Chapter Eleven
Grandpa

Hannah can't sleep. She lies in the darkness, eyes
wide open. She hears the drainpipe flapping in the
wind against the bathroom wall. The flapping
monster, Sue called it when they were all little and
they dived under the blankets and blocked their
ears. Even now, when Hannah hears the knocking,
tiny shivers run to her toes and she gathers the
blankets tightly.

Lena and Sue on the other side of the room
breathe together. Together they roll over and the
bunk creaks and groans. Hannah can just make out
her books back on the shelves, her soft toys on the
box at the end of her bed. Rain falls softly on

the roof and on the broad leaves of the plants outside her window.

Hannah's foot twitches and butterflies hatch in her tummy.

How could they laugh? Have they told Grandpa? How can she look at him tomorrow? She sits up.

She needs a drink. She rolls quietly out of bed and feels her way to the door. Her toe kicks hard against a plastic rollerblade. Then she's in the hall. Tiptoe, past the telephone table, past Mum and Dad's door, past the bathroom. Ahead is the kitchen. The door is closed but a sliver of light seeps from under it. Has someone left the light on? Are Mum and Dad still up. Hannah stops, listens. No sound. A cat yowls outside. Maybe Mum is there rocking Megan, trying to settle her down from a bad dream. Maybe Mum, by herself, will understand.

Hannah pushes the door open.

Grandpa is at the table, feet up on a chair in front of him, a cup of tea by his elbow. The snowdome with the Harbour Bridge is beside the sugar bowl. He nods to her so she cannot run away. Eyes down, she crosses the room to the sink and pours a glass of water. What can she say? Good morning? But it's the middle of the night.

Lovely weather? But it's raining. Can I help you back to bed? Does he know what she's done? Has Dad told him?

'I can't sleep,' whispers Hannah.

'Me neither.'

He's in his pyjamas. Blue and yellow stripes, faded from washing. A few white chest-hairs straggle through a gap in the front where he has lost a button. She sits down opposite him. He picks up the cup and blows on it. Steam floats across to her. The fridge hums. The clock ticks.

'You don't like me being here, do you?' he says.

'No.' Hannah's voice is small. She looks up at him. His eyes are pale, watery blue. The skin around each eye is gathered in wrinkles but still it seems so thin that the slightest touch might tear it.

'I don't like me being here either.'

Silence. Humming. Ticking.

The rain has stopped.

'You've been trying to get rid of me, haven't you?'

So they have told him.

Hannah nods.

'I'm glad.'

'Glad?'

'You're the only person in this house who doesn't treat me like a baby, like an invalid. Everyone has been so *nice*.' He curls his lips and the word hisses out and lands with a slap on the table.

'I've got everything they think I need; twenty-four hour care, love and attention and all in that fresh new room. Your room.'

'The best room in the house,' whispers Hannah.

'I don't want it,' says Grandpa. 'It's not mine.' He sips his tea, replaces his cup and then sits back with his hands in his lap.

'You see, Hannah, when you're sick you spend lots of time in bed, thinking. It's best to be where you've done things. Where things have happened to you. Your room's lovely, but it doesn't mean anything to me. I need to be where my ghosts are.'

'Ghosts?'

He grins. 'Friendly ones. Not scary ones. Memories. That sort of thing.'

'So where do you want to be?'

'Home. My room doesn't have the fresh yellow ceiling that yours does, that you chose, but I've been lying in my big bed looking at that ceiling for fifty years or more. I don't care if there's mould in the corner where the water used to come in. I don't care if the curtains need a wash and the walls are different colours because your grandmother and I could never agree about the paint. I think of her whenever I look at the pinkish-brown that she said was mushroom and I thought was yuk. I can feel her in that room with me, but here . . .' He shakes his head and for a minute Hannah thinks he's going to cry.

'She didn't make the trip here with me.'

He picks up the snowdome and shakes it so that it is filled with whirling flakes. 'We used to take a walk across the Bridge every Sunday. It was our special outing. She found this in a junk shop, years later. I think of her every time I pick it up.' He places it gently on the table. 'I think of her when

I look at you, too. You're very like her.'

'What will you do?' Hannah almost whispers.

His shoulders sag. 'I don't know. Be brave,
I suppose.'

Brave? Brave is when you fall off your bike and
there's gravel in the cuts on your forehead and it
stings and Dr Mark says he has to clean it out.
Every single bit.

'Your father is determined to take care of me.
He doesn't want me to go home. He says it would
be brave and foolish. I don't see it that way. I'm
not brave, Hannah, and I have to be brave if I
stay here.'

Chapter Twelve
Family Conference

*H*annah hates family conferences. She sits at her seat at the table and watches the others. 'Everyone gets to speak,' says Dad. 'And everyone will listen and not interrupt.'

Last week, it was pocket money for jobs that hadn't been done and whether Lena and Sue should help Hannah feed Ceefer, and if not should the TV be turned off. This week it is how we can all live more easily with Grandpa.

Grandpa is watching the news. He doesn't know that people are talking about him at a family conference.

Mum taps the table with her fingernail. 'We're

having this talk,' she says, 'because Dad and I are really upset at what's been going on. We know it's hard having Grandpa here. It's not easy for any of us.'

Hannah is watching the stream of ants that comes up from the space at the back of the stove. The straight line heads across the pale-green kitchen bench, past the coffee plunger, past the wooden breadboards till it reaches the compost bucket. Orange peel and honey toast crumbs have spilt from the container. The ants swarm over these and then, clutching tiny fragments, stream back the way they came.

It was Hannah's turn to wash up. It was her job to wipe down the benches. She saw the crumbs and the peel and she saw the advancing ants. One swipe of the dishcloth and they would all have gone down the sink.

She couldn't do it. She picked up the carrot scrapings and wiped the spilt tomato sauce.

She mopped the splashes of water on the bench and carefully skirted the ant column.

'Hannah's the one causing all the trouble,' says Lena. 'Just talk to her.'

'That's not the solution,' says Mum. 'You two aren't being very kind to Hannah. It's not her fault that she didn't move into her new room. You aren't the only ones who can complain. Dad and I have still got Megan in our room, too. We were looking forward to having her move out to be with Hannah.'

'You never get cranky with Hannah,' says Lena. 'If Sue and I did what Hannah's done, you two would just go off your brains. We'd be in the biggest trouble and you'd ground us forever. What happens to her? Nothing.'

'That's not true,' says Mum. 'We'll deal with Hannah in good time.'

'Well, how long is he going to be here?' says Sue.

Dad shrugs. 'We don't know. He's far from well. He can't live on his own.'

'He's not going to stay forever, is he?'

'Listen, Sue,' says Dad, 'I don't think you kids have any idea what it's like to be old. Your grandfather has been sick. He's still sick. He can't look after himself. What he needs is love and care and people around him who are his family. You're all to help him and be nice to him for as long as he's here.'

'That's right,' says Mum. 'It isn't all that difficult. As Dad says, just make him feel he's part of the family. Be nice to him.'

'He doesn't want you to be nice to him.'

'What?'

'He doesn't want to be here.'

'Don't be ridiculous, Hannah.'

'It's true. He says his ghosts aren't here and he'd rather be looking at the mould on the ceiling in his old bedroom like he has for fifty years and he doesn't want you looking after him and he's got to be really, really brave if he stays here and he doesn't feel brave and he hates people being nice and I think he's feeling really, really sad.'

'Of course he's not happy,' says Dad. 'He's a sick man.'

'I don't think that's what Hannah means,' says Mum, quietly. 'Have you been talking to your grandfather, Hannah?'

Hannah nods. 'Last night. And it's all true. You ask him.'

'I think we should,' says Mum.

It's pitch dark. Hannah wakes to the sound of
Megan crying. Footsteps and low voices. Hannah
gets out of bed and goes along the hall to the
kitchen. Mum is pacing up and down, patting
Megan on the back and singing softly to her,

'A jolly little workman,
Was making toys one day
So children could be happy
When they were all at play . . .'

'You woke me up,' says Hannah.
'Sorry. Blame Megan.'
Hannah tickles Megan's bare feet.
'Nah, nah.' Megan reaches out across her
mother's back.
'She's saying *Hannah*,' says Mum. 'I think she
wants to go to you.'
Hannah sits down and takes Megan on her lap.
She holds her close and pats her back.
'Say Hannah,' she says.
'Nah, nah.' Megan snuggles up against Hannah's
warm pyjamas.
'Dad and I have had a long talk to Grandpa,' says
Mum. 'You're quite right. He doesn't want to be
here. I had no idea he was that unhappy.'
'Can he go home?'

'As soon as he's well enough. We'll get him a
nurse to visit and some home-help with cooking
and cleaning.'

'Is Dad happy about it?'

Mum nods. 'He came round in the end.' She
strokes the top of Megan's head. 'She's asleep at
last. Let's go back to bed.'

'Mum,' says Hannah, 'I didn't say what I said
about Grandpa because I wanted the room.
I really didn't.'

'I know, love. I know.'

Chapter Thirteen
The Tomorrow Room

*T*he tomorrow room is empty. Only the bed, stripped of sheets and blankets, stands against the wall. Hannah and Annie stand in the doorway.

'Has he really gone?'

Hannah nods. She feels strangely empty too. Like she's lost something and she's not quite sure what it was and she knows she'll never find it. 'He didn't go because of me, though. He wanted to.'

Grandpa left that morning. He went with Dad, back to his house. Someone from the council was going to meet them to talk about meals-on-wheels and a district nurse who would pop in every day

to check that he was all right. He had a new wrist
bracelet that had a transmitter in it. If he had a fall,
he could press a button and his doctor would
know he needed help.

'I'll be OK,' he said to Mum and he kissed her
on the cheek. 'Don't you worry about me.' He
leant on his new stick. It had a top on it like a
duck's head and he pointed it at Megan and said,
'Quack. Quack.'

Lena and Sue stood together at the gate. 'See
you,' he said. 'Thanks for being nice to me and
putting up with me.'

Hannah walked with him to the car. Dad fussed
around tucking a blanket over his knees. When the
door was closed, Grandpa wound the window
down and reached out for Hannah's hand. 'I'm
going to miss you,' he said. 'There's a present for
you. Your mum's got it. It's from me to say thank
you.' He squeezed her hand. 'See you.'

'See you,' she said.

Hannah works all day with Annie.

'You get your present when the room's ready,' says Mum.

So Mum calls Peter from the house on the corner and together they move in Megan's cot and the red chest of drawers. They drag in an old bookcase that Dad has stained and Mum puts hooks on the back of the door for anything that needs hanging. She gives Hannah a soft, rag rug that her mother gave her when she left home.

Hannah and Annie sort out the books. Cardboard ones for Megan to tear go on the bottom shelf with the soft toys and blocks. Hannah's books go on the top. They find sticky stuff for the back of last year's birthday cards, the class photo and the certificate for being a ripper reader and they press them onto the wall above the bed. 'I'll come back tomorrow and see what the present is,' says Annie when she has to go home in the middle of the afternoon.

Hannah sits Megan on the rag rug in the middle of the room. Between them is a brown parcel, the present from Grandpa. He's gone home to his friendly ghosts, to his room where things have happened to him.

Will things happen in her room? Will there be friendly ghosts for her?

She looks down at the parcel. Is Grandpa her first ghost? She can almost fesel him with her. Hannah tears the paper off and hands it to Megan who scrunches it into a ball.

'Megan the Pegan,' whispers Hannah. Her little sister laughs and holds the paper out to her.

'Look, Megan. Look!' Hannah rips open the small grey box and lifts out the snowdome.

How could he? It was so special.

She shakes and shakes it. Megan drops her paper
and reaches out.

'Nah, nah.'

Hannah puts an arm around her little sister,
drawing her close.

'My turn first,' she says. 'Then yours.'

Laughing, they fall back on the soft patterned
folds of the rug as the snowflakes swirl and swirl.

About the Author

Libby Gleeson has taught in secondary schools and tertiary institutions in Australia and overseas. She is now a full-time writer and her award-winning novels include *Eleanor, Elizabeth, I am Susannah, Dodger, Love Me, Love Me Not* and *Refuge*. Libby's first book about Hannah was *Skating on Sand*. This was followed by *Hannah Plus One*, which was the winner of the 1996 Family Award for Children's Literature (Younger Readers), and the 1997 CBC Book of the Year Award for Younger Readers. Libby lives with her husband and three daughters in Sydney.

About the Illustrator

Ann James taught art in secondary schools and then worked as a designer and illustrator of educational books and magazines while establishing herself as a freelance illustrator. Ann has illustrated many books for children, including the Mrs Arbuckle books by Gwenda Smyth and the Penny Pollard books by Robin Klein. In 1988, she and Ann Haddon established a gallery for children's book illustration – Books Illustrated. Ann lives in South Melbourne with most of the cast from her book *Finding Jack*.

Other books in the *Hannah* series available in Puffin

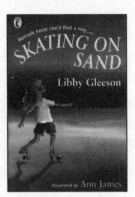 

SKATING ON SAND

Skating is what Hannah wants to do most, and she is not going to take her skates off until she can skate without falling over. But everyone in the family says it can't be done . . .

HANNAH PLUS ONE

When Hannah learns her mum is expecting another baby, she is convinced it will be another set of twins, leaving Hannah the odd one out. It's a time to strike out and stand up for herself because soon Hannah too will be a big sister.